Raising Yoder's Barn

BY JANE YOLEN

PAINTINGS BY BERNIE FUCHS

LITTLE, BROWN AND COMPANY
Boston New York Toronto London

My brothers and I worked hard all summer
in a field with furrows
straight as a good man's life.
Our sickles swung against the wild mustard
that crept in on the growing grain.
It was the first summer
Papa let me cut alongside my brothers.
"Matthew," he said to me,
"I can see that you have good hands."

Little Sister ran back and forth
from the spring house,
a white water jug in her hands,
trying to keep us cool at our work
under the blazing summer sun.
But I hardly felt the heat,
as I grasped the handle
of the long cutting blade
proud to be beside my older brothers,
proud to have such good hands.

Then one Monday in July turned angry and dark.
Black clouds scudded across the sky.
Lightning, like a stooping hawk,
shot straight down toward our barn
and struck the windmill on the roof.
That windmill gave us power
for the corn sheller,
for the feed grinder.
Papa liked to call that windmill
"God's own right hand."

Fingers of flame grabbed at the barn.
The sky filled with blue ropes of smoke;
a boy could climb them up to Heaven,
if he were so willing.
The cows were not tied in their stalls,
so they ran out the barn door and down the road,
bawling all the way
till our good Amish neighbors took them in.
Papa, Elam, and I carried buckets of water
to the side of the burning barn.
Joseph, David, and Jacob were on the roof,
bringing up the buckets with ropes.
Soon the palms of my hands
were covered with pearly blisters,
like the barley in Mama's soup.
Grandfather ran from the Dawdy Haus to help,
shouting instructions in a voice
made harsh by the smoke.
Christian, being the youngest,
rang the bell long and hard to summon the neighbors.

The neighbors heard the alarm and came:
some in wagons,
some on horseback,
most on foot.
They formed two long bucket lines,
and Mama and Little Sister pumped
until their own hands were raw.
We saved the house,
but no one could save that barn,
though it had stood first before all
on our farmland.

Tuesday, soon as it was daylight again,
we surveyed what remained.
The old timbers were still smoking,
"Like an old man at his pipe," Papa said.
A poor joke, but still we laughed.
Disaster makes even the lamest joke funny.

Sore hands or no,
we raked the ashes out the next day,
and Christian painted his face with them.
Mama was not amused,
and attacked his face with a wet cloth
till his cheeks were red as flames.

The neighbor men came to walk around the cellar hole,
talking in soft voices about fires.
"I recollect the one that took the Widow Lapp's home."
"There was one got the old schoolhouse."
"And the fire that ate up Miller's silo."
They knew — we all knew —
that a farm is not a farm without its barn.
A barn for the cows,
for the hay in winter,
for the keeping of goats and hens and chickens,
for the tools in their proper order.
Barns come first
on a proper Amish farm,
even before the house.
At last someone said, "Call Samuel Stulzfoot.
It is time for a frolic.
It is time to raise Yoder a new barn."

Samuel Stulzfoot came Thursday in his buggy.

He was a minute of a man,

small and dark and wiry,

but he could build a big barn.

"He's done so many," Mama said,

"he can see them in his head."

Samuel Stulzfoot stepped out the boundaries twice.

He tapped on the timbers to see if any could be saved.

Then he turned to Papa and smiled.

"Clear her" was all he said, and was gone.

By day's end, with all of us working hard,

the clearing away was done.

And early Friday morning, teams of men
hauled in beams and boards and wooden pegs.
Wagons of women and children arrived,
loaded with hampers of food.
"Raising Yoder's barn!" cried one small boy,
leaping down from his wagon,
so excited he ran back and forth
like a dog after hens.

Soon Christian and other boys joined in the chase.
I was excited, too.
I had been to many barn raisings in my eight years.
But this was the first one on our own farm.
I was hoping Papa would think me
old enough to really help,
me and my good hands.

Elam and David were sent to work with the hewers,

Jacob and Joseph with the carpenters.

Christian and the little boys

scoured the ground for fallen things:

nails, hammers, bits of boards.

But I was too old for them.

I waited to be told, waited for Papa's call.

Waited while the first of the frames

was ready to be hauled into place.

Would Papa never notice me?

Would I have no job to do?

I was big enough for scything.

Surely I was big enough to work on our new barn.

Then I felt a hand on my shoulder.

I turned around

and there was Samuel Stulzfoot,

his eyes narrowed, as if he were thinking.

"My throat is hoarse," he said.

"I need a boy just your size

to carry my instructions to all the workers.

Will you do it?"

Would I do it!

My voice would be as good as my hands.

I scrambled over boards,
climbed up the sides of beams,
ran around front side to back,
backside to front,
bringing Samuel Stulzfoot's words
to all the working men.
And sixty feet by forty feet,
to the sound of many hammers ringing,
that barn grew like a giant flower in the field
all in a single day.

At noon we ate on the trestle tables,
a holiday meal served up by the women:
soup with dumplings,
ground meat sausages,
pickled cabbage,
potatoes and applesauce,
apple butter slathered on fresh baked bread.
But even such good food
Could not keep us long from our work.

The barn was finished before dusk
with the new moon rising behind it.
"A new moon and a new barn," Mama said.

After the neighbors were gone,
back to their own farms,
Papa gathered us all by the barn door.
"We cannot thank the Lord enough
for such good neighbors and such good friends.
But each time we go into this good, plain barn
it will be a blessing."
"Amen," said Grandfather.
"Amen," the family replied.
"Amen," I whispered,
for I had no more voice than that, even for a blessing.

At harvest time, Papa's blessing proved true.
Hay dripped over the barn's low beams.
The cows stood contented in their new stalls
while Little Sister, her cap slipped back off her head,
pulled down the hissing milk into the shiny pails.
"A blessing indeed," I said out loud,
looking over the tools in their proper places:
axes and hoes, shovels and rakes.
And there, along with the rest,
my own scythe stood, its blade newly honed.
It was waiting patiently for the summer,
when once again it would fit comfortably
into the palms of my good hands.

AUTHOR'S NOTE

When my husband and I lived and worked in New York City, we used to rent a car on weekends and drive down into Amish country in Pennsylvania. We loved the rolling countryside, the beautiful farms, the sight of the Amish in their horse-drawn buggies. I knew that either we would live there someday or else I would write about that landscape and those good people when I found the right story to tell.

This is that story, about an eight-year-old Amish boy named Matthew Yoder, and what happens when fire destroys his family's barn. The Amish say, "A good barn built made many a fine house." In fact the Amish always build the barn first, and when the farm is successful, a good house follows.

The Amish are a particular religious group who live in yesterday. They reject cars, public electricity, colorful clothing, television, computers, movies — in fact most of the things that we take for granted as part of modern life. They are a dynamic, hardworking people who are committed to a Christian community. One of their beliefs is that neighbors must help neighbors. Entire Amish communities will get together to raise a new barn. Typically, that barn goes up in a single day.

The names Yoder, Lapp, Stulzfoot, and Miller are all Amish names. A "Dawdy Haus," or grandfather's house, is where the grandparents live after they have gone into retirement, leaving the running of the family farm to the next generation. It is not at all unusual to find several generations of an Amish family all living and working on the same farm.

TO MARIA, WHO RAISES BOOKS, NOT BARNS —J.Y.

FOR ZAZIE — B.F.

First Edition

Library of Congress Cataloging-in-Publication Data

Yolen, Jane.
    Raising Yoder's barn / by Jane Yolen : paintings by Bernie Fuchs. — 1st ed.
      p.   cm.
    Summary: Eight-year-old Matthew tells what happens when fire destroys the barn on his family's farm and all the Amish neighbors come to rebuild it in one day.
      ISBN 0-316-96887-0
      [1. Amish — Fiction.   2. Neighborliness — Fiction.   3. Farm life — Fiction.]
    I. Fuchs, Bernie, ill. II. Title.
    PZ7.Y78Ra1 1998
    [E] — dc21   97-13101

10 9 8 7 6 5 4 3 2 1

SC

Published simultaneously in Canada by Little, Brown & Company (Canada) Limited

Printed in Hong Kong